Revamped

a love story

SHARON
KIZZIAH-HOLMES

Publishing Coordinator – Sharon Kizziah-Holmes

Paperback-Press
an imprint of A & S Publishing
Paperback Press, LLC.
Springfield, Missouri

ISBN -13: 978-1-960499-45-5

DEDICATION

To the memory of my niece, Shannon.

With love to Cary.

CHAPTER 1

Shannon followed the real estate agent, Hayley, up the stairs to the door of the old frame building. It was just what she'd been looking for. She had always wanted to live in a small town, and right in the middle of Jonesville Township was the ideal place for her antique shop.

"Oh, and there's an added bonus to this property," Hayley said. "The river runs just behind the building, and there's a great view out the back."

"That sounds wonderful." The peacefulness would surely heal the scars on her heart. It had been almost a year since her husband's fatal car accident, but living in the home they'd shared had been too much of a reminder of his abuse. He said he loved her, but if that was love, she wanted no part of it. The words 'I love you' were empty. They were meaningless now.

No one knew of his cruelty toward her, and she'd vowed to keep it to herself, especially now that he was dead. Even though she still cherished Austin, Texas, the move would be the best thing for her.

She studied the structure. It had been well cared for, and the huge windows in front would be just right for her displays. She watched the agent place the key in the wooden framed door that held an old piece of stained glass in its center. She loved the place already and hadn't even been inside.

Hayley pushed the door open and the sound of a tiny bell that hung above the doorway drew Shannon's attention. She shivered and rubbed her arm, surprised goose bumps had risen. How odd. She glanced at the bell and determined it belonged right where it was, and if she decided to buy the property, it would keep its place.

"I see you're admiring the doorbell, Miss Rhea."

"Yes, it actually gave me cold chills when I heard its sweet chime. It's beautiful."

The woman smiled and walked to the

center of the main room. "Dane has been here since the original owner hung him in that spot over a hundred years ago."

"Oh?" Shannon inhaled as deep as she could to take in all of the scents in the space around her. The musty smell of old, the aroma of cedar, and a faint hint of perfume or cologne filled the air. But the bell, she couldn't get the sound out of her head. "Why do you call the bell, Dane?"

"That's his name."

"Let me get this right. It's a boy bell with the name, Dane." She thought it silly the thing had a name, but she wanted to hear the story behind it.

"Yep."

She brought her gaze back to the tarnished brass object. "Tell me about it, please."

"Well, this building was built and owned by some folks from England. They were a middle-aged couple who had been successful in their country but wanted to see if bigger and better things awaited them in the U.S. They brought their life savings to build and run their shop."

Fascinated by the history of the building, and even the story of the couple, Shannon listened while she walked around the room checking the built-in shelving in the walls. "What kind of shop did they have?"

"They had things imported from their homeland and made this an Old English market. Dane belonged to the woman's grandmother who was from Denmark.

"What were the original owners' names?"

"Clifford and Willena." The woman hesitated. "Oh, my gosh!"

Shannon turned toward Hayley. "What? What's wrong?"

Hayley rubbed her arms. "Now *I* have goose bumps."

"Why?" It got cold all of a sudden. Maybe not cold, but the air seemed definitely cooler. What was going on?

"Cliff and Willie, their last name was Rhea, spelled exactly like yours."

Her heart skipped a beat. "Rhea?"

"Yes."

Could it be that fate had led her to a building her deceased husband's ancestors built? Why? Now she wished she'd paid more attention to his family history. "Those names don't ring a bell." She glanced at Hayley and started to laugh, which echoed throughout the empty building as if to multiply in intensity. Apparently, Hayley hadn't noticed the strange resonance of the laughter as it faded.

The agent walked to the door. "They don't ring a bell, huh. No pun intended, right?"

Dane released his musical sound again with

the door closing, and this time it warmed her instead of making her shiver. Almost like it welcomed her, but how could that be? It was a bell for heaven's sake. Now her imagination was getting the best of her. "No pun, trust me." She might do some research on his family tree. It was intriguing to think his relatives could have built this. "Now, tell me more about Dane." Calling a doorbell by name was madness! But it felt natural.

"Dane is a good luck piece and once he was mounted, he's never been moved. On Cliff and Willena's wedding day in the 1850's, Willena's grandmother gave the bell to her so it would ring her granddaughter a prosperous life. It worked, and when the Rheas moved here, they named the bell Dane, which means, from Denmark, like Willie's grandma was."

"Wow, that's so interesting." She met the red-haired agent's gaze. "How come you know so much about this place?"

"I've lived in Jonesville all my life. My mother is from here originally, and after she and Dad married, they stayed.

"My father, Ben Jones, was the township's historian. Having the name Jones, as in Jonesville, is just a coincidence. Anyway, he worked in this building when he was a young man, and so did my brother. It was an antique shop then, too. Come to think of it, since the

Rheas have been gone, it's always been an antique shop.

"However, it's been empty for some time now. The township has maintained it pretty well."

Shannon studied the shiny hardwood floors and clean interior of the shop. "Yes, I'd say someone has. May I ask why it's been empty?"

Hayley chuckled. "It's silly, but some say that after Willena passed away, Clifford felt her presence here, and now that he's gone, it's thought that they are both here in spirit."

Haunted? She swallowed hard and thought of the sudden change she'd felt in the air earlier. In all of her twenty-six years, she'd never believed in ghosts, and she wasn't going to start now. However, it fascinated her. "You're right, that is silly."

Stepping toward a closed door, Hayley said, "I agree, now would you like to see the apartment upstairs?"

"Yes, I love the idea of living above the shop. So far, I couldn't have built a place more suited for me if I'd done it myself."

"I'm glad to hear it." Hayley opened the door and led the way up the stairs.

All Shannon could think of was how would she ever get her furniture up there? "These are so narrow."

"There's an outside stairway, too. It leads to the main entrance of the apartment. I think you'll like it. There's a beautiful deck that was added on a few years ago, so you can walk out your front door and look right at the river. It's really peaceful out there. Now, this door opens into the kitchen," she said as she opened the door at the top of the stairs.

Shannon liked the thought of having a door at the bottom and top of the stairs. That made the apartment more private in a way. She entered the small kitchen and instantly fell in love. "This is so cute." Even though it was empty, she imagined her belongings placed around the area.

Glass front cabinets lined the walls and light-colored counter tops lay beneath. The refrigerator wasn't full sized, but she didn't need anything bigger, and the undersized four-burner gas stove fit neatly in its cubby hole. "How adorable, I love it."

"Wait 'til you see the rest."

When they entered the living area, she knew she was home. A large picture window allowed the sun to brighten the room and when she looked out, the river ran less than 100 feet away. Wild honeysuckle climbed the trunks of towering oak trees. She opened the door that led to the large wooden deck and inhaled the sweet aroma. Her decision was made. "I'll take it."

"But you haven't even seen the oversized claw-foot bathtub yet."

"Claw-foot bathtub? Now I know I'm in heaven. Let's get on with the paperwork. I'm ready to move in and get my business started." Dane rang from the floor below, or was she hearing things? "Did you hear that?" she asked Hayley.

"What?"

"Dane."

"No."

"Well, I think someone just came in downstairs." She went to the stairway and headed down with Hayley behind her switching off lights along the way.

Upon entry into the main room of the shop, all was quiet. Why had she thought she'd heard the doorbell ring? Was it her imagination again? Was this place really haunted? No. She glanced up at Dane, and he slightly swayed back and forth. Surely the bell hadn't rung by itself.

"What was that?" Hayley asked.

Shannon jumped and her heart threatened to burst out of her chest. "What the…?" She turned toward the direction where the door had slammed. To her surprise, a man stood behind them. Was he a ghost?

CHAPTER 2

Hayley put her hand to her chest. "Cary, what are you doing here? You scared the hell out of us."

"Sorry, I was just double checking the work I did in the storeroom. I saw your car and knew the door would be unlocked, so I came on in."

The man stood at least six foot three. He was distinguished looking with his slightly graying, sandy brown hair. It had been a long time since Shannon had seen someone with a flattop haircut, but he wore it well.

He looked familiar. Did she know him?

She stepped toward him and admired his muscular frame. His jeans didn't fit too badly either. "Hi, I'm Shannon." She offered him a handshake.

The man accepted her gesture. "Cary, ma'am."

Heat rushed up her arm, through her veins and to her very core, but she didn't let go of his grasp, nor did she want to. "Have we met somewhere? I sense that I know you." A strange feeling bubbled up inside her. Who was this man? His smile didn't hide the unsure look in his beautiful green eyes.

"I get the same feeling, but I can't think of where it might have been."

"Well, it's nice to meet you." He held her hand just a little too long, but she still couldn't pull away. Her skin tingled where he touched it, and the scent of cologne she'd admired earlier was now more present in the air. Damn he smelled good.

She gazed into his eyes and saw kindness there. Familiarity? But that wasn't logical. When he released his grasp on her hand, she shivered, missing the warmth of his touch.

Cary put his arm around Hayley's waist when she stepped up next to him. "How are you doing, babe?" he asked.

"Great now that you're here." Hayley stood on her toes and gave Cary a peck on the cheek.

It was clear Hayley and Cary were close. The look in the other woman's eyes showed she had high admiration for the tall man, maybe even love. She felt ridiculous for having such an immediate attraction to him when it was obvious he and Hayley were a couple.

Hayley's attention once again came back to Shannon. "Cary is the mayor of our township."

"Mayor, I'm impressed." Actually, she was more than impressed with his status as mayor. She was *totally* impressed with him and understood why Hayley was so enamored. She, however, should have no interest, not after what she'd lived through the last couple of years of her marriage. She had to remember a man in her life was the last thing she wanted or needed.

Cary smiled. "Well, don't be too impressed. I don't really have to do anything since our town almost runs itself. I just wear the name. I make my living doing carpentry, building furniture and collecting and restoring antique pieces. Are you thinking about joining our little community?"

"Yes. I think I will."

"So, you're buying this old, haunted shop?" he asked with a chuckle.

Somehow it seemed like he belonged in the building. The way he looked at the structure made it clear he loved it. "I believe I will buy it, but I don't believe in hauntings, Mr…?"

"Just call me Cary." He dropped his arm from Hayley's waist. "That's good to know. It will be nice to have a new, beautiful face in Jonesville."

What did he think was so good to know? That she was joining the community or that she didn't believe in hauntings. She didn't care, besides, was he flirting with her? How rude, and right in front of his girlfriend. Maybe she just thought she was impressed with him.

Then why, if she didn't approve of his actions, did he cause her heartbeat to run away with itself? His smile showed straight white teeth, and a warm breeze seemed to pass between them when he stepped closer. Another temperature change, how weird.

"What are you going to do with this wonderful old place?"

She met his gaze. Suddenly, the warmth overwhelmed her, and she was uncomfortable in his presence. Not uncomfortable, maybe, comfortable? Whatever, she didn't know what it was but something wasn't right.

The air seemed statically charged between her and the man in front of her. She took a step back, but an unknown entity pulled her closer. It wasn't a physical pull, more like something inside her. An emotion she'd never felt before.

A lump formed in her throat, so she swallowed hard and forced back the feelings. Maybe it was simply because she thought he was attractive. That had to be it. Anything else was unacceptable. He belonged to Hayley.

She thought back to the question of what she was going to do with the building. "My husband and I owned an antique shop in Austin." She had always loved antiques. Her husband, on the other hand, never had and blamed her for every little thing that went wrong.

He had been the one who wanted to own a business. It wasn't her fault he'd insisted on opening the shop. But he'd known if it was something she loved, like antiquing, she would do all of the work, and she did. So, it was her fault for allowing him to use her that way. At least it kept her busy and away from him part of the time. She had to stop thinking about it, it was over.

The real estate agent smiled. "Husband? You didn't tell me you're married."

She wouldn't have been surprised to hear a slight bit of relief in the other woman's voice. "No, Hayley, I didn't because I'm not, I'm a widow."

"My condolences." Hayley paused. "Then, that would mean Rhea is your married name?"

"Yes. My maiden name is Kirby. I was going to take it back when Peter was killed, but for some reason I changed my mind."

"Killed? Oh, that's awful."

"Time's making the pain better. It's been almost a year since it happened. After the car wreck, I closed the store. Now I feel I should move on." She glanced around the room that seemed so familiar. What had drawn her to this small community? "I still have most of my inventory. I love antiquing, and this will be a great shop."

Cary said, "It's interesting your name is Rhea? That name means a lot to the township. I'm sorry about your husband, but I assure you, you'll love it in our little town of five hundred."

"Wow, five-hundred." She enjoyed hearing his voice. It was deep, smooth, and it soothed her in a way, but she couldn't bring herself to look him in the eye again. "That would add up to one subdivision in Austin." She was pleased when they both laughed. She wasn't sure, but she hoped she'd get out of there with little or no more uneasiness, or whatever it was she experienced in Cary Jones' presence.

If her first encounter in the small

community, with a person other than Hayley, made her have feelings entirely alien to her, maybe she'd been too hasty in her decision.

Hayley stepped toward the door, her laughter subsiding. "But, Shannon, a subdivision in Austin doesn't have the character Jonesville Township does."

"You're right about that." She took a quick look around the room, then thought about the small apartment above. She couldn't allow a womanizer like Cary, whoever, to dissuade her decision. However, she would do some soul searching to find out why she was even attracted to the man when he was spoken for.

She took in her surroundings once again. No, this was home. She belonged here. One thing she now knew for sure was that the Rhea Building would be hers.

Cary reached for the doorknob. "Maybe we can get together soon." He met Shannon's gaze.

Get together? How dare he ask her out right in front of Hayley. If nothing else, his arrogance should help her fight any feelings she could develop for him if he *were* available. "I doubt it. I'll be very busy getting settled." He smiled that perfect smile, and she found herself lost in his gaze. Why did she feel like she knew him?

"Maybe after you get settled, I can come in

and see if you need some pieces refurbished."

She had to break the spell he was casting on her. "Thank you, sir, but I do my own restoration."

"Cary, Shannon and I better get going to the office," Hayley said. "We have a lot of paperwork to do."

"Okay." He opened the door. "Will I see you at the house later?"

"Yeah, about six."

"You know what to bring."

Shannon was almost embarrassed to hear the personal conversation between lovers. Especially, after he'd tried to make a date with her. At the same time, she felt the pangs of jealousy stab her heart. She watched Cary bend and give Hayley a hug and a loving kiss on the forehead then heard the woman's words.

"Only for you, my darling, only for you."

CHAPTER 3

Cary drove toward home and couldn't stop thinking about the woman named Shannon. Her long blond hair had been fashioned in a soft braid down her back with short tendrils wisped around her face. Her blue eyes sparkled in the sunlight that filtered through the big windows of the old building, and her hand was as soft as velvet when he clasped it in his.

The uncanny notion that they'd met before still lingered in his mind. Wracking his brain, he couldn't figure out why he knew her, but he did. Next time he saw her, maybe it would ignite a spark of recollection as to where they'd met.

He understood why she wouldn't accept his proposal to get together. She probably had misunderstood what he'd meant. He wasn't actually asking her on a date, was he? No, his offer was for companionship since she didn't know anyone in Jonesville, but it was probably too soon after her husband's passing for her to consider it.

How stupid of him not to think about that before he asked, but even if she didn't want to go out, he'd thought surely she'd be interested in doing business with him. Oh well, nothing he could do about it now. He only hoped that the old Rhea building didn't get to her as it had to everyone else who'd ever owned it besides Cliff and Willie. What a coincidence her name was Rhea, too. That puzzled him. Could she be related to the original owners? Then he remembered that was her deceased husband's name. He didn't care what her name was, as long as the old building would be occupied again.

It had sat empty for many years before the last tenants took it about ten years earlier. They kept it the longest, but still, they left a couple of years ago. It was a beautiful structure and added so much to their little township, but the things that happened there were too much for folks to stand.

Why had he never experienced any of the hauntings? He'd been in there for hours by himself and felt nothing but comforted. At home really, but that wouldn't happen now. His thoughts to buy the property and open his own shop were swept under the rug by the new girl in town. His pulse quickened at the thought of the warmth her touch spread throughout his body. How could a mere stranger have that effect on him? Was she a stranger?

Taking a deep breath, he pulled into the parking lot of Franklin's. A cold drink sounded like the perfect thing to wet his whistle.

He studied the outside of the establishment, then glanced up and down the main street. He loved this little town. Even after he'd moved to the city, he longed to come home. Something drew him to the small community, and it was an easy decision for him to come back to help take care of his mother. After his father died, it was too much for his sister to take care of the house, their mom and work at the same time.

"Hi, Cary, want your regular root beer float today?" the waitress asked.

"No, Cassie, I think I'll just have a root beer, no ice cream."

"Are you on a diet or somethin'?" She glanced at him and chuckled.

"Just big plans for supper tonight and I want to leave room."

"Oh, I see."

He watched her set the bubbling brown liquid on the counter and put a straw in it. "Hey, Cass, your grandpa here?"

"Yep, he's cooking today. Want me to go get him?"

Cary glanced around the empty room and smiled. "If he's not busy."

She laughed. "You came in at just the right time," she said, as she went into the kitchen.

He sipped on his soda and admired the nostalgic soda fountain setting. It had been the same for the last sixty or more years. Even the old hanging lights were original and well cared for.

It pleased him to know the residents of Jonesville took pride in the appearance of the township. It helped to bring tourists in during the summer season. It was a treat for visitors to be able to shop the quaint businesses and float the river, too.

The older man entered the room, wiping his hands on a crisp, clean white apron. Johnny Franklin had been Cary's dad's best friend, and he found himself turning to Johnny for advice more times than not. "Hey, you old fart. You run everyone off with that grouchy attitude of yours?"

"Old fart? You watch your manners young man. I can still take you out behind the shed." He took a seat on a barstool.

Cary sniggered. He loved the old guy. "It wouldn't be the first time, but I bet I can outrun you now."

"Don't be smart. What brings you here today? No doubt you're seeking my advice because of my abundant wisdom."

"You are big-headed aren't you, ol' man? Matter of fact, I brought news."

"Oh, probably something I already know."

"That Hayley's going to sell the Rhea building to a beautiful young lady? Did you know that?" He could tell he'd piqued Johnny's interest and concerns. He met the man's gaze and nodded.

"Hmmmmm, interesting. We'd better get a booth and talk about this." Johnny got off his stool. "Cassie, would you bring me a cup of coffee, please?"

"Sure, Papa John."

Cary picked up his root beer and followed John to the booth. "I know what you're thinking."

"Damn right. That place should be torn down. Too many weird things happen in there. I'll put a hundred on the table she won't stay through tourist season."

He thought about Shannon and the strength in her beautiful blue eyes. Besides, she said she didn't believe in ghosts. What the hell? "Okay, you're on." Just the thought of tearing down the building made his blood run cold. It was a historical mark in Jonesville and he loved it.

John took his coffee cup from his granddaughter. "Thanks, baby girl."

"Welcome," she replied and walked away.

"Who is this woman?"

"An antique dealer from Austin."

John shook his head. "Another antique shop going in there. Does she know it's haunted?"

"Yep, and she still wants it. You know, I've been in there many times and have never had any encounters."

"You're too all fired mean for any ghost to want to mess with you."

"Hey, now, that's not fair." The soda tingled on its way down, then he placed his glass back on the table. Ice clanked against the glass as he moved the brown liquid around with his straw, knowing full well it didn't need stirring. "Actually, she said she doesn't believe in ghosts."

"That'll change. Does she know that both Clifford and his wife died in that apartment?"

"I'm not sure about that. I'll ask Hayley tonight when she comes over."

"She'd better be totally up front with the lady before they sign any papers. I'd hate for the woman to have to sell out and run like the others have."

It was true; Shannon deserved to know all the details about the haunting, or whatever it was. "You're right. I'll call and tell Hayley that." He reached for his cell phone and pressed Hayley's quick dial number. One thing he couldn't stand the thought of was losing Shannon, the woman he loved. What the hell? Where had that come from?

CHAPTER 4

"Hello?"

Shannon tried not to pay attention to Hayley's phone conversation as she studied the documents in front of her. She only hoped the owners took her offer. It was at the low end of what she could afford, so if they made her a counteroffer, she'd be in the position to counter again if needed.

"No, not yet, but we're about to make an offer... Why? I didn't think about it... I guess you're right... Yes, I'll do it now... Okay... I love you, too, see you tonight... Bye."

She couldn't help but hear what Hayley

was saying, so she assumed she'd been talking to Cary. She thought back to his bright smile and kind eyes and her heart skipped a beat. He was all she'd ever wanted, but how could she know that? She'd only seen him one time. So, why did she feel like she knew him?

What was wrong with her and why was she thinking about him when she was doing business with his sweetheart? *You must be losing your mind!* She had to shake the memory and get on with the deal. "Do you think they'll take this offer?"

"It would be nice if they did."

Hayley fidgeted and squirmed in her seat. Shannon was puzzled by the look on the woman's face. Apparently the phone conversation had been about her buying the building and she felt she had the right to ask. "Was that your boyfriend? Is something wrong?"

Sitting back in her chair, the agent said, "My boyfriend? No, that was Cary."

"Well, I thought..."

The woman began to laugh. "You thought Cary was my boyfriend? That's hilarious," she stated between guffaws.

Now Shannon was totally confused, but the other woman's amusement was contagious. It seemed like such a long time since she'd really let go and laughed but now it came easy.

She finally caught her breath. "Boy, that felt good, but why is that funny? I mean, at the shop he kissed you and told you he loved you. And don't you two have a date for supper tonight?"

Hayley wiped tears from her eyes. "Yes, I guess I can see where you might think that, but Cary is not my lover, he's my brother. Our date is at our mother's house. Cary helps me take care of her, and every Saturday night we get together at her place for supper. Cary's a great cook."

Shannon's heart leapt in her chest and her stomach did flip flops. They weren't lovers! Thinking back on the encounter, she couldn't figure out why she'd read more into it than was there. Was she trying to protect her own heart? "Your brother? Boy, I feel like an idiot." At least now she didn't have so much guilt about the thoughts and feelings she'd been experiencing.

Shaking her head Hayley said, "Don't, there was no way you could have known. Cary's the most single man I know, and he's going to laugh his butt off when he hears this."

"You don't have to tell him."

"Oh, yes I do, this is classic. Just like your little shop's going to be, Shannon."

Now that she thought about it, it would be nice for him to know because he might ask her out again. She found herself truly smiling about both Cary being single and making the offer on the shop.

"Maybe we'd better move on with making the bid." Again, she noticed the concerned look on the agent's face, and she remembered the phone conversation the woman had had with her brother. "Is there something about the deal you're not telling me?"

"No, not exactly." Hayley hesitated. "Well, kind of. I guess before we make your offer, you need to know a little more about the haunting at the Rhea building."

It sounded funny to hear Hayley call the property 'The Rhea Building', but she loved the sound of it almost as much as she loved the building itself. However, she was troubled that the alleged haunting had become more of an issue. "What about it? I told you I don't believe in ghosts."

"My brother," Hayley said and smiled, "thought you should know the full story behind it before you make your final decision."

At least Shannon knew Cary was thinking about her. Could he really be interested? Why was she allowing herself to imagine these things? It didn't matter if he was interested or not, she wasn't, or at least she didn't want to permit herself to be. But with Cary it was hard, there was something about him that made her want to know him. Every inch of him. "That was nice of your brother. Go ahead, tell me more."

"It may not make any difference to you, but both Cliff and Willie died on the premises, actually, in the bedroom of the apartment."

"No, that doesn't bother me in the least. People died at home in those days." Then why did she feel a sudden sadness?

"At times, after Willena passed, patrons would catch Cliff talking to himself. He claimed he was talking to Willie."

Shannon didn't think that was so unusual. "I have to admit that after my husband was killed, I spoke to him sometimes, but I didn't think he was actually there."

Hayley sat back in her chair. "Well, the difference is, Cliff thought his wife's spirit was with him all of the time. He professed he could see her now and again.

"After Cliff died, the second owners couldn't handle the fact that they would hear a man's voice in the building when no one else was there. Then items in the shop would get moved from one place to another or disappear altogether.

"They decided to sell when the wife

thought she saw the figure of a woman standing over her in the bedroom. When she got up, the apparition was gone."

Unable to believe what she was hearing, she began to laugh. "That's the most ridiculous thing I've ever heard. Ghosts standing over the bed, things disappearing because a ghost took them, it's crazy."

"Not big things disappeared," Hayley continued, "just small items, but all were valuable pieces from England. Most had belonged to Cliff and Willie and somehow found their way back to the shop only to mysteriously vanish."

Shannon didn't know why they were even having this conversation. "You know as well as I do, Hayley, that those things most likely walked out the door with some customer that was too cheap to pay for them."

"I have to admit you're probably right, but that's not all. After those folks sold out, the next few owners missed items and heard the voices, too. Dane would ring in the middle of the night. It seemed he held a key of some sort, because if they heard him in the night, they knew something would be missing, or moved, in the morning."

"Well, there you go; someone was coming in and taking it."

"No, no one was there. Many times they

would go immediately and check. The door was locked and no one was inside."

Thinking about what the woman had said, Shannon came to a conclusion. "There has to be a logical explanation for these things happening. Did anyone ever find any of the stolen items?"

"Not a trace."

"What about the folks I'm buying the building from? Were they scared away, too?"

"Not frightened away, no. The folks you're buying the property from didn't let a lot of that bother them. Actually, they didn't have much haunting after they moved in. It just so happened they were from England, too. We all wondered if that made a difference to Cliff and Willie. The Crawford's stayed a few years."

Surely Hayley didn't believe in the haunting, but from what she had just said, she did. Shannon reminded herself that she didn't believe in such things, so nothing like that would happen to her, but now her curiosity was piqued. "So, why did they leave?"

Hayley sat forward and put her elbows on the table. "As I told you, the Rhea building has always, for some reason, been an antique shop.

"The Crawford's had gone to Dallas to an auction. They bought a box of goods but didn't see all of the individual items that were included. You know how auctions are when they sell in bulk to liquidate."

Shannon knew exactly what she was talking about. She'd bought bulk at auctions before.

"Anyway, after the couple got back to the shop they began to go through what they'd purchased. They found a small wooden box, and inside it, wrapped in a silk cloth was an old set of gold wedding bands. They were thrilled."

"Yes, I would have been too."

"They figured the set dated back to the mid eighteen hundreds. With further inspection they studied the rings with a magnifying glass and what they found engraved inside the bands astonished them and everyone in Jonesville."

Enthralled with Hayley's story, Shannon hadn't, until now, noticed she was sitting on the edge of her chair. What was the woman waiting for? "Come on, tell me. What was engraved on them?"

Hayley cleared her throat as if it was hard for her to say the words. Tears welled in her eyes and Shannon felt sudden warmth around her. "Don't keep me in suspense, Hayley. What did the rings say?" The warmth turned to a chill and she shivered.

The agent inhaled deeply then exhaled. "Clifford and Willena."

She hadn't realized she'd been holding her breath until she released the air in her lungs and sat back in her chair. "What?"

"Yes, they were the Rhea's wedding bands."

"What a coincidence. Why would that make the Crawfords leave?"

"That's not what did it; they placed the rings in the same glass cabinet that's still in the building."

"The one against that back wall?"

"Yes, it belonged to the Rhea's originally. That old display case was where they locked the bands up and showcased them, with no intentions of selling the pair. It was like an historical event here in town. Everyone was so thrilled that part of Clifford and Willena was back, they flooded the shop admiring the rings. After about three weeks on display, the gold bands disappeared."

Why would someone do something like that? It was beyond her how some people had no conscience. "How did it happen? You said the case was locked, didn't you?"

Hayley nodded. "It was, with the original lock the Rhea's had used. It is very old and there is only one key. The lock stays with the case. It's in the shop right now."

Shannon swallowed the lump in her throat as she watched the woman walk across the room to a little safe. Hayley opened the secure box and took out a small satin bag. The moment she shut the door to the lock box, Shannon noticed a musty smell in the air. What was it?

She knew exactly what it was. The feeling she had when the other woman handed her the satin bag was something she'd never experienced until then The key, somehow she felt it belonged to her. Why did she feel it was something she'd had forever and she'd missed it? She closed her fingers around the soft holder and felt the metal object inside. "Thank you for giving this back to me." The look on Hayley's face made her realize what she'd said.

"Pardon me?"

What was happening? None of this made sense. "I-I don't know why I said that." She saw Hayley shiver.

"I don't either, but for a minute it gave me the creeps."

"Finish your story, please." Shannon glanced down at the hand that held the key. Why hadn't she realized she was grasping it so tightly? Her knuckles were white from the pressure. She opened the bag, removed the key and put it on the desk top. It looked brand new.

Hayley sat in her chair once again. "No one could comprehend how the rings had vanished into thin air. There was no evidence someone had been in the cabinet or the shop. The rings were just gone."

She couldn't believe it. "Did the officials dust for fingerprints?"

"Yes, nothing."

"How bizarre." Could it be that all of these peculiar things actually happened because of a haunting? No, that was ridiculous, and she refused to allow herself to think about it. Even though her personal experiences so far had been, in the least, different, and the way the key felt in her– No!

"Yes, bizarre. Now you see why we thought you should know everything. The Crawfords decided that was the last straw. They were like you and figured someone local was stealing from them so they are selling out."

"May I ask how long they have been gone?"

"About two years. They left just before my father passed away." The woman cleared her throat. "Now, if you change your mind, I'll understand."

Shannon nodded; she would definitely have to think about this now. However, what was there to think about? She loved the place. It was exactly what she'd been looking for and all she had to do was install cameras. If someone secretly got into the shop, she'd have them on video and the mystery would be solved.

Smiling at Hayley she said, "I'm not changing my mind because there's a thief around. Hopefully, they got what they wanted and won't come back to the scene of the crime. Let's make that offer."

She picked up the key and returned it to its satin bag. It was all she could do to force herself to hand it back to Hayley. It wasn't hers, and logic told her it never had been, but somehow, she felt it had. She would have to be satisfied to know that if the deal went through, the key would be hers again.

CHAPTER 5

Cary enjoyed having the top down on his classic nineteen fifty-seven Ford Fairlane. His Saturday afternoon drive brought him into town to pick up some things for his mother, but all he could do was think about Shannon Rhea.

As he passed by the Rhea building, he glanced at the store front. Shannon had named her shop Revamped and the new sign was hung. The windows were again full of displays very tastefully done. She was not only beautiful, by the looks of the designs, she was talented as well.

It had been a month since she opened her doors and, even though it seemed something drew him to the place, he hadn't been inside. As hard as it was, he'd forced himself to stay away.

The more he'd thought about the old Jonesville Township's historic Rhea Building, the more he realized he'd always been particularly fond of it. Even as a boy he'd loved it, and his first job had been working for one of the previous owners. That's where he'd learned so much about antiques, though it seemed the knowledge came naturally.

When he'd been renovating parts of the structure before Shannon bought it, he noticed how comfortable he felt. He would love to visit her now and see what she'd done to the inside. He wouldn't mind seeing the prettiest woman in town, either. However, invading Shannon's privacy was something he didn't want to do.

Amusing as it was that she thought he and Hayley were lovers, she'd made it clear she wasn't interested in him, or any man for that matter. He decided to give her enough time to settle in before he went to see her new business and officially welcome her to Jonesville.

The few times they had seen each other, which was inevitable in the small township, the meetings were friendly. Though he'd said cordial hellos and gone about his business, the strings of his heart tugged a tighter grip of interest in the woman. Something he'd never felt before. It was more or less like he'd always known her and maybe even... loved her.

Wanting to get involved in a relationship after his last one miserably failed, was something he didn't think he'd do for a long time. There'd been something missing with every woman he'd dated, but Shannon Rhea was different, there was something about her that intrigued him.

She was so young to be a widow and must have been very in love with her husband. He figured it would take her a while to get over her loss. However, every time their gaze met, a spark ignited between them. No, not just a spark, a force that bonded them in some way. He couldn't figure it out but found himself wanting to pursue a relationship with her.

Thoughts of blond tendrils framing her face and big blue eyes gazing up at him entered his mind. He glanced in his rear-view mirror and watched the shop growing smaller in the reflection. "Oh, the hell with it!" He turned his car around and parked directly in front of Revamped.

Now was as good of a time as any to greet her. Why was he putting it off, and why was he making excuses to do so?

He felt like a high school boy afraid to ask a girl to the prom. He had to keep it in his mind that all he wanted to do was welcome her to town. It was his job as mayor.

That wasn't the reason at all. Even with all of his inner turmoil about the situation, his past girlfriends, and Shannon's recent loss, he still wanted to spend time with her.

Dane jingled when he opened the door and stepped inside the small shop. His heart skipped a beat when he saw Shannon working on a display across the room. How could he feel like he was in love with a woman he didn't even know? He swallowed hard, surprised at how nervous he truly was. "Hi."

Shannon jumped when she heard a man's voice and turned toward the sound. "Cary." She felt awkward for some reason, but at the same time exhilarated he was there. She'd been wondering when he was going to visit, but she didn't know butterflies would invade her stomach when he did.

Why hadn't Dane warned her someone had entered? She pushed strands of hair away from her face toward her braid. "I didn't hear you come in."

"Sorry if I startled you." He glanced around the shop. "The place looks great! You've got some really nice pieces."

His smile made her tingle inside. She walked toward him and offered a handshake when she really wanted to put her arms around his neck and kiss him. "Thanks."

He grasped her hand. "It's good to see you."

The static in the air made the hair on back of Shannon's neck stand up. Why did this happen every time she got close to this man? But most of all, did he notice it? She realized he did when he quickly withdrew his hand.

"It's good to see you, too." She hadn't realized until that moment she'd missed him. Why did she feel as if Cary was a loved one who had finally returned home from a journey?

It was hard to tear her gaze from his, oh so memorable, eyes. She felt she knew them by heart and had looked into their depths for a lifetime. What was it about him that made him so familiar? She forced herself to look away. "Well, er… come on in and look around."

He turned and strolled through the store, studying its contents. "How've things been going?"

"So far, so good." Better now that he was there, but she wouldn't tell him. "I love my little shop. It feels like home."

"No weird encounters? Nothing coming up missing or anything?"

She chuckled. "No, not yet, but I was wondering why Dane didn't ring when you came in."

Cary glanced her way. "He did."

"He did? Well, I didn't hear him, and I usually hear him every time the door opens. So, I guess that's the first weird thing that's happened." She enjoyed hearing Cary laugh.

"I see you put the Rhea's display case back in its original spot. I'm glad Hayley told you where it went."

Shannon shook her head. "No one told me to put it there, that's where it belongs." Cary rubbed his hand along the edge of the glass, but what she saw in his eyes was more than admiration. "It's a beautiful piece of furniture, isn't it?"

Cary nodded. "Yes, I've always loved it, and you're right, it belongs right here." He met her gaze. "So do you."

Heat of passion blazed in his eyes. Why did she feel like she'd been there before? She placed her fingertips to her lips when the warmth of a kiss brushed against them, but Cary hadn't kissed her. Her mind was playing tricks she didn't understand.

This time, she couldn't force herself to look away from his mesmerizing green eyes. He stepped closer. Close enough the heat of his body penetrated her clothing. Then he took her in his arms and she didn't object because it felt right, natural. But how could she know that?

"Shannon, I—"

Within a heartbeat he bent and pressed his lips to hers. Everything faded around them and her world was in this man's embrace, his kiss. Was it her heart she felt beating, or his? It was as if they were one and had always been.

She didn't want it to end. An unexplained emptiness invaded her when he slowly ended the kiss and stepped away, passion and longing still evident on his face.

What was wrong with him? The overwhelming desire to kiss the beautiful woman in his arms was more than he could control. The last thing Cary wanted to do was let her go, but he had to. He had no right to overstep his boundaries.

He forced himself to release her lips when all he really wanted was to kiss her longer, deeper, make love with her. It was all he could do to step away from her warmth. He fought to catch his breath. "I-I don't know what came over me. Please forgive me."

The flush of her face made her more beautiful than ever. He loved the way she pushed the loose curls away from her face and wondered what she'd look like if all of her hair hung loose across her shoulders.

"Forgive you?" She turned and walked away. "I don't remember protesting what just happened."

"No, I guess you didn't." He smiled and remembered how she'd leaned into him, welcomed his kiss, even acted like she wanted more. The feel of her breast pressed against his chest caused blood to rush to his groin. He had to leave before he took even more advantage of the situation and kissed her again.

She was facing the window and her hair glistened in the sunlight. He desperately wanted to reach out and touch it. How had this woman captured his heart so quickly? Had she been there all along? Was she the one he'd been waiting for?

He'd known for a long time his soulmate was out there somewhere. Now she was here. He felt it to the core of his very being.

He approached her from behind and placed his hands on her shoulders. Her breath caught, and he knew she felt the same charge of energy he had.

Dare he turn her around? No, he was

having enough trouble controlling his emotions without seeing her beautiful face. "Shannon, I don't know what's happening between us, but you and I both know it's something beyond our control. You feel it, don't you?" Her nod gave him affirmation.

"I don't want to go, but I need to." He dropped his hands and she turned to face him. Her blue eyes filled with want and questions.

The warmth of Cary's arms, the feel of his lips, his taste, was everything Shannon knew it would be. "Yes, I think you need to go, too."

She had to compose herself. What was happening between them? Whatever it was she was afraid of it and loved it at the same time. Damn the man for making her love him. Love? That was impossible. She'd seen him all of maybe a dozen times, so why did it feel like she'd known him forever? "I appreciate you coming by, though."

Cary stepped toward her and her breath caught in her throat. Was he going to kiss her again? She wanted him to more than anything, but Dane rang out a warning that someone had entered the shop. They backed away from each other, and she wondered if they looked like a couple of kids caught with their hands in a cookie jar. She smiled at the thought and glanced at Cary who had a wide grin.

"What are you smiling at?" he asked.

"What are *you* smiling at?" She couldn't believe it when simultaneously they both said, "Cookie jar". His laughter filled the room, and she couldn't help but join in as she walked beside him toward the door.

"Would you consider having supper with me tonight? I'd love to introduce you to my mother. Hayley will be there, too."

Before she had time to think, her heart compelled her to say, "Yes, I'd like that."

"Great! Pick you up at six."

"I'll be ready." She opened the door and Dane rang out happily. That was absurd, how could his ring sound any happier than it always did? Watching Cary walk to his car, she struggled with the urge to run after him, but the realization that she'd see him again in a few hours made the need bearable.

CHAPTER 6

Shannon glanced at her reflection in the mirror for about the hundredth time. The jeans and white cotton gypsy shirt she'd decided to wear were comfortable, but was it a suitable outfit for supper? Mostly she wondered if it would please Cary.

A knock at the door brought a sudden stop to her observation and made her blood rush with anticipation. She glanced at her watch. Six o'clock on the dot. At least he was punctual.

She walked from the bathroom across the living room to the door. Placing her hand to her throat, she wondered if her heart was going to stop. The doorknob was cool to the touch, unlike the heat that rushed to her face when she greeted the most handsome man she'd ever seen. "Cary, hi, come in."

"I'd better not. I wouldn't want the enchiladas to burn."

She turned the lock in the knob, stepped onto the deck, met his gaze and closed the door. "What's that supposed to mean?" His eyes smoldered with suggestion.

"You know full well what it means."

She did, and it excited her to think about being in his arms, naked, making love. "Mmmmm, I love the thought... of enchiladas that is."

"So do I, and I'll bet they'll be the best in the state of Texas. I make a mean green sauce. I hope you like chicken, they're my specialty."

"Absolutely love chicken enchiladas! They're my favorite."

"Now, how'd I know that?"

She, too, wondered how they knew so much about each other. Maybe she really didn't know it, but it was in the back of her mind that he loved milk. She shook her head. What a silly thought.

Though it didn't take long for them to get through town, she enjoyed the drive to his mother's home. They rode in comfortable silence.

He pulled onto a long gravel drive then stopped once they passed through the entrance of the property. She watched his muscles flex as he got out and closed the gate.

She was fascinated by the energy that passed between them when they were close to each other. How could being around him seem so natural in such a short time? Was there something unexplainable about the two of them and their pull to each other?

As they moved toward the house she was awed by the surrounding area. They approached from the back, and she could see the home was built into the side of a hill. Both stories were visible from behind, but in front it looked like it was only one floor.

Cary got out, went to her side of the car and opened her door. The sun was still visible over the tall trees of the wooded yard. The smell of lilacs drifted through the air and she was at peace. "This is beautiful."

"Thank you. It belonged to my grandparents. My mother's lived here almost all of her life."

She followed Cary into the house. Once inside, the open floor plan allowed her to see into the kitchen. She breathed in the aromas of fresh salsa, green chilies and chili powder.

"Wow, if this food tastes as good as it smells, you might be right about it being the best in Texas."

"Hi, Shannon."

Hayley came out of the kitchen wiping her hands on a small towel. She was such a beautiful woman and Shannon loved the color of her hair. Her green eyes were the same color as her brother's, and just as kind. "Hi. It smells great in here." She glanced at the redhead's apron then at Cary. "I thought you said you made the chicken enchiladas."

"He did," his sister said. "I saw y'all drive up so I was just getting things on the table. I'll just finish up while you meet Mom."

Cary took her purse and placed it on the end table next to the couch. "See how quick you are to think I would story to you?" he said.

A lie would never leave his lips. He was the most honest man she knew and she would trust him with her life. There it was again. That uncanny feeling they'd known each other for years.

Shannon heard footsteps from the hallway behind her. She assumed it was Cary and Hayley's mother, so she turned to greet her.

"This is my mother, Pat. Mom, meet Shannon, she bought the old R—"

The smile Shannon had faded when she

49

saw the look of shock in the older woman's eyes and the color drain from her face.

Cary rushed to his mother's side. "Mother? Are you all right?"

She wouldn't stop staring at Shannon. "I-I need to sit down, that's all."

Cary helped Pat to a chair and Shannon saw the woman was trembling. She hadn't even said hello to her. Surely she didn't dislike her already.

"What happened?" Hayley went to her mother's chair. "Mom, you're as white as a sheet. You look like you've just seen a ghost."

Why wouldn't the woman stop staring at her? She wanted to run from the scrutiny, but with further study, she saw no ill feelings in her eyes. But there was something akin to disbelief. Shannon swallowed the lump that had formed in her throat and forced herself to breathe.

Cary took his mother's hand. "Mom, tell us what's wrong." He followed the woman's stare. "What is it? This is Shannon, the woman I told you about."

Before he turned his attention back to his mother, Shannon saw worry in Cary's eyes. Pat blinked a few times then averted her gaze, and Shannon was glad for the reprieve. However, the deep frown that creased the woman's brow did little to boost her confidence.

"I guess I just got faint from hunger. I'm sorry." She took a deep breath. "I'll be fine, really, just give me a minute to sit here." She glanced once again at Shannon. "Honey, forgive my manners. Welcome to our home."

"Thank you. I'm sorry you're not feeling well."

Cary stood and she longed to take his hand for moral support, but she didn't have to, he took hers. She wondered what was going through his mother's mind each time she looked at him then back at Shannon, as if she knew something they didn't.

"You two make a handsome couple indeed. I knew the right woman would find my son one day. I believe that day is here."

"Mom, please, we hardly know each other."

Pat smiled. "Yes, but you feel like you've known each other for a lifetime. Am I right?"

"How could you know that?"

"Ah, mothers recognize these things, dear."

Shannon gazed into Cary's eyes ,and the charge that usually passed between them was stronger than ever. She remembered Cary's words from that afternoon. Could he be right? Was what was happening between them something that was beyond their control?

Hayley cleared her throat and broke the hex

that bound her brother and Shannon. "Well, shall we eat before mother has another spell, or her intuition tells us more than we want to know?"

CHAPTER 7

Cary put his car in gear and drove through the gate toward the highway. He glanced over at Shannon and saw the confused look on her face. "Penny for your thoughts."

"Oh, I was just thinking about the things your mom said this evening."

"Do you think she's crazy?"

"No, don't talk like that. It's just—"

"Just what?" He took her hand and rubbed his thumb across its softness. Her skin was like satin under his touch. He longed to take her in his arms and protect her from what was bothering her. However, he knew what was on her mind. It had been on his all evening.

"Do you remember what you said today at Revamped?"

"About things being beyond our control?" He remembered it well and felt it in his gut. Something was pushing them together.

"Yes."

He momentarily met her gaze, then turned his attention back to the road. She was so beautiful it took his breath away. His whole being was filled with her.

"What if you're right? I mean, I sense it, here." She pointed to her heart. "I've never felt these emotions before or the strange electricity that passes between us."

They couldn't have this conversation while going down the road. There was a scenic point just around the next curve. He wanted to look into her eyes while they talked. This could be the most important discussion of their lives.

Shannon was pleased Cary pulled off the road. She was afraid of what might come to pass between them. Not that she was scared they would actually fall in love, but that they wouldn't. Maybe her feelings were just lust, not love at all.

The thought chilled her to the bone. Never in her wildest dreams did she think that in six weeks' time, she'd meet the man of her dreams, fall in love and feel like their affections had always been.

Cary put the car in park and turned off the headlamps. The parking lights were still on, which allowed the dim glow of the instruments in the dash to illuminate the car's interior. She studied his features in the soft light. He was so good-looking it made her ache for his touch, but that wasn't all that attracted her. It was his heart, his eyes, his whole being, that filled her with want. He turned toward her and his large hands gently engulfed hers.

"I don't know where to start," he said. "All of my life I've been drawn to the Rhea building. I've been fascinated with it and I know almost every nook and cranny of it." He smiled. "Matter of fact, I was about to make an offer on it, but you got there first."

"I'm sorry. Didn't Hayley know you wanted it?"

"No, I never said anything to anyone. I only made the decision the day before you looked at it. And don't be sorry, I think you love that old building almost as much as I do."

"I do love it, very much." She loved him, too, but those words wouldn't come so easily even though she wanted to blurt them out. His smile warmed her heart as did the sincerity in his gaze.

"The minute I walked in today, I knew the right person owned the property. Everything is as it should be inside, just as I remember it."

The faraway look in his eyes reminded her of what had happened to her when the feeling of déjà vu overwhelmed her. "Remembered it from when?" When he was a boy? When they were married? This was a ridiculous conversation, she didn't believe in any of it. However, she couldn't deny the emotions that had reeled through her since she'd been in Jonesville Township.

"Well, I'm not quite sure. It's almost like it was in another lifetime."

A cold chill ran up her spine, and Shannon couldn't stop the shiver as it made its way to the surface. She turned and faced forward. "May we go please?"

"Why? We need to talk about this."

Now anger began to seep into her mind or was it fear? Fear of glancing into the unknown. She'd let all the talk about hauntings and ghosts get to her. No, she would not stand for these silly thoughts to occupy her psyche any longer. "Really? Talk about what, Cary?"

"Us and what's happening between us."

She met his gaze once again, but this time she tried to keep her emotions in check. "What's happening between us is we're attracted to each other. You're a man, I'm a woman. It happens all the time." Did she really believe that?

"Being attracted to someone has never affected me like this. Has it you? Have you ever experienced the feelings we get when we touch, the static in the air when we're together inside the Rhea building? Haven't you wondered why we feel like we've been there before?"

She had never told him any of these things. "How do you know I feel the same things?"

"Sweetheart, don't try to fool me. I know you like the back of my hand. See, that's what I'm talking about. Why would I say that? Unless—"

She was really starting to get uncomfortable with all of this. "Unless, what? We were re-incarnated as someone from the past destined to be together no matter what? That's just stupid, Cary." She couldn't handle any more of this nonsense, but she couldn't deny the feelings she had either. "Take me home, please. I don't want to talk about this or think about it for one more minute."

CHAPTER 8

You could have cut the tension with a knife for the rest of the ride back, and she hated it. Why was she being like this? She loved this man and now she was pushing him away.

Cary pulled to the back of the Rhea building, and she stepped out of the car. Glad to be back in the fresh air, she inhaled a deep breath.

She felt as if Cary's gaze burned into her backside as he followed her up the stairs. "You don't have to walk me to the door. I'm perfectly capable of getting inside myself."

Why the hell hadn't she remembered to

turn the porch light on? She fumbled through her purse for her keys, relieved when she touched their cold metal. The light of the moon was just enough to let her put the door key in the lock.

"Shannon, please."

She opened the door and stepped inside. When he tried to follow, she placed her hand against his chest. She couldn't refute the volt of energy that coursed through her, but she chose to ignore it. "Conversation over, Cary. I don't believe in ghosts, reincarnation or hauntings. I never have and never will. I will admit there have been some strange coincidences, but that's just what they are, coincidence."

"But—"

"I'm tired and I'd like to go to bed." She looked into his beautiful green eyes. The sadness she saw in them all but broke her heart. Why couldn't they have just had a normal relationship like other people? She couldn't let this go on. The words all but stuck in her throat, and she fought to get them out. "Please, don't come by for a while. I need to get my thoughts composed."

"Don't turn me away like this. We're bound to be together."

"Just give me some space, please."

Nothing in Cary's life had been so hard as to leave Shannon, get back in his car and drive home. He couldn't understand why she was being so closed minded about their relationship. Yes, it was farfetched, and he had never believed in anything like this before, but damnit, his feelings were too strong.

It had been only minutes since he'd dropped her off, but to him it seemed like hours, even days. He didn't want to be away from her for a moment, but she'd made it clear she needed her space. He was a man of his word, so he'd give it to her.

His mother had acted so strange all evening. It baffled him how she knew the things she did. He was going to find out exactly why she kept staring at him and Shannon throughout the whole meal.

He closed the gate, got back in his car and pulled into the garage. The attic ladder was down, and light shown from the opening to the garage floor. It had been years since he'd been in the small space.

Reaching the foot of the ladder, he looked up. "Mom, are you up there?"

"No, Cary it's me. She asked me to get this

old trunk down, but I can't lift it. Would you help me?"

Why would his mother want Hayley to get a trunk from the attic this time of evening? "Sure."

Cary pulled the oversized suitcase to the edge of the ladder. "I'll go down and you slide it over the side. I'll grab it and take it in."

It was heavier than he thought, but he managed to get it to the ground without much trouble. "Did she say what this is all about?"

Hayley opened the door leading into the house. "All she said was there was something we needed to know and she didn't think it could wait any longer."

"This was Dad's army trunk."

"I know," Hayley replied. "I remember when we used to go through it and look at his old pictures. That was a lifetime ago and before he put this lock on it."

At the mention of 'a lifetime', his thoughts went back to Shannon. "Shannon was freaked out by the night's events. She doesn't want to see me for a while. Said she needs time to get her thoughts together."

"Can you blame her? After what Mom said, and the way she stared at the two of you all night, it made me want to crawl under the table."

"I guess it did Shannon, too." He glanced

down at the battered green trunk. "We'd better get this inside and find out what this is all about."

Cary's mother sat in her favorite chair, the key to the trunk rested between her fingers. "Mom, are you okay? We don't have to do this tonight. It can wait till tomorrow." Tears welled in her faded green eyes, and he realized for the first time, she looked tired.

"No, son, it can't wait." She bent and placed the key in the lock.

The clank of the metal latch hitting the side of the trunk echoed in the quiet of the house. He watched as Pat slowly and carefully opened the lid. Inside, his father's dress greens lay right on top. His mother began to talk.

"You kids know how much I loved your father, don't you?"

He and Hayley both answered with a nod. His mother and father's love for each other had been evident all of his life. Their love was true, and that's what he had hoped to find.

"Cary, I know how much you've always loved that old Rhea building. It's in your blood. Your father and I have known it for a long time."

"Yes, but what does that have to do with Dad's army things?"

"Now, don't hurry me. It's taken me a long

time to tell you this." She sat back and folded her hands in her lap.

Watching the thoughtful look on his mother's face made Cary even more curious. It was all he could do not to prompt her to continue.

"You know, you might be right." Pat leaned forward, closed the lid of the container and placed the lock back in its place.

Now he was more confused than ever. "Right about what?"

"This can wait until tomorrow. I've been keeping this secret a long time. One more day isn't going to matter." She closed the lid, locked it, then stood and put the key into her pocket. "When the young woman opens tomorrow after lunch, we will take the trunk to town, to the Rhea building. Shannon should hear this, too."

"That won't work, Mom." Cary took a seat on the couch. He would like nothing more than to see Shannon again.

"Of course, it will work, darling."

"She doesn't want to see me for a while. After tonight she's confused and..." He paused and his heart skipped a beat. He knew what was wrong with her. "And, frightened." He glanced up in time to see his mother smile in understanding.

Pat touched Cary's hand. "Absolutely she's

frightened. Most people are scared of what they don't understand, and some want to deny the existence of the inevitable."

Somehow, he knew exactly what her words meant. However, he'd never seen her act this way before and his mother's mental state worried him. Hayley's voice drew his attention and her words told him she felt the same way.

"Mom, are you sure you're feeling all right?"

The older woman nodded. "I feel fine, dear. Tomorrow it will all be clear to everyone, and I'll feel even better after that." She turned and walked down the hallway. "Goodnight, my precious children."

Cary looked at his sister and she shrugged. He then glanced at the trunk. What could its contents hold that would bring all of these strange happenings together? One thing he knew for sure, Shannon was not going to be happy when she saw them walk through the door of Revamped.

CHAPTER 9

Shannon glanced at her watch. One o'clock, time to open the shop. She stepped to the door and turned the lock. The beautiful Sunday afternoon prompted her to prop the door open. The fresh air would do her good after the sleepless night she'd had.

She couldn't get Cary, and everything that had happened, off her mind. The things he'd said, even if she didn't want to face the reality, actually hit home. However, instead of making things clearer, it put questions in her mind.

Why had she been drawn there? She'd never heard of Jonesville Township, but when she looked at the area map for a small town to move to, the name immediately drew her attention. Now that she thought about it, the name all but popped out and hit her in the face.

Damn, why hadn't she realized before now she hadn't even considered looking anywhere else? Also, why did she fall in love with this building only to find out it was called the Rhea Building?

Shannon hadn't thought Rhea was that common of a name. Could it have been an unknown force that drew her here? And what about the immediate feelings she had for Cary. There was love at first sight, at least she'd heard of it, but this was off the charts!

It all made her doubt her own beliefs. Her mother had believed in the supernatural, but her father had always instilled logic and the supernatural wasn't logical. Was it? No. So why did everything point to – "Oh, stop it!" Her mind told her none of it could be true, but her heart told her she and Cary were destined to be together.

A car door closed outside and voices filtered in. She glanced up and saw the man of her dreams. She had told him she didn't want to see him, but he hadn't listened. With each fiber of her body, Shannon wanted to be angry, but as soon as she saw him, all that melted away.

She watched him open the trunk of his car and retrieve an old army box. Her breath caught in her throat. He looked so strong, handsome, and so damn sexy it made her yearn to be in his arms. Why did every emotion she had surface when she saw the man?

Surely the visit was business. Why else would Hayley and Pat have come along? Did they want to display something in her shop, maybe something in the trunk? She took a deep breath in through her nose and released it slowly out her mouth. It didn't help, her heart still beat wildly. "Focus." Yes, she would force herself to keep her focus on business and not on Cary.

Why was she trying to lie to herself? Business was the last thing on her mind. Seeing Cary, even though she tried to convince herself otherwise, was first and foremost.

A warm breeze rushed through the door just before Cary entered with the old trunk. Dane jingled as if sending out a welcome greeting. *It was the breeze that rang the bell, Shannon. The bell didn't ring itself.* "Logic," she whispered under her breath.

Cary sat the trunk on the floor beside a small seating area she had for her customer's comfort. He stood to his full height and glanced at her. Embers of passion glowed in his eyes when she met his gaze. The electricity in the air, she'd almost become accustomed to, sparked between them and threatened to steal her breath.

"Shannon. I'm sorry for coming after you asked me not to, but Mother insisted."

She broke the trance he held over her and greeted her guests. "I-it's okay. Hayley, Mrs. Jones, it's good to see you." The warmth of Cary's hand on her shoulder radiated through her body and rested in her heart.

"We need to talk, privately."

It made no sense, but the last, and the first, thing she wanted to do was be alone with this man. She glanced up at him trying not to focus on his green eyes. "Now? It looks like your mom has business we should take care of."

"Now, please."

The look in his eye told her something was very important to him. "Okay, let's go to the storeroom."

They walked side by side, and she remembered the first time she ever saw him. He came out of the very room they were about to enter. She flipped on the light switch and turned toward him. "Is something wrong?"

If she had wanted to protest his kiss, she wouldn't have had time. His lips were warm and inviting, and she leaned into him. She knew at that moment she would be with Cary Jones forever. It was meant to be, one way or the other, and she was tired of fighting the truth. She was his, mind, body and soul.

He released her lips but held her close. She placed her arms around his waist and snuggled against him. Safe and loved is how she felt. His chest vibrated and tickled her ear when he spoke.

"I had to do that. I missed the hell out of you. I know you didn't want to see me again for a while, but—"

"Shut up. I'm glad you're here." When he chuckled, she couldn't help but smile. God she loved him.

"You are?"

She leaned back and gazed into the eyes she'd come to know so well. "Yes, I couldn't stop thinking about you last night, and when I saw you out front, I wanted to run away and at the same time, run into your arms."

"I thought of you all night, too. I love you, Shannon. That's all I know that's real about the chain of events over the last few months. I have fallen in love with you."

The three words she never thought would mean anything again, now meant the world. "I love you, too." Had she really professed her love? Yes, and it felt great! "I love you. I love you! There, I said it. Out loud and everything, now are you happy?" His smile caused butterflies to flit through her.

"The happiest man in the world."

Her heart sank when his eyes grew serious. She knew he was going to get to the real reason he'd wanted to talk to her in private.

Cary cleared his throat, dropped his arms and took Shannon's hands in his. "I don't know what's in that trunk out there, but whatever it is, my mother thought it important enough for us to be together to see it."

"Where did it come from?"

"It was my dad's. It's been in the attic. He put a lock on it a few years before he died. I never knew why, but I have a feeling we're fixing to find out."

"Then I guess we'd better get back to your mom and Hayley before customers start to come in." She turned toward the door leading into the shop.

"Shannon?"

Stopping at the sound of his voice, she didn't face him. "Yes?" His arms encircled her from behind, and she placed her hands over his, welcoming his embrace.

"No matter what happens, we are here for each other, we can't forget that. Right?"

Swallowing the lump in her throat, she nodded, frightened to learn what was in the container, but excited at the same time. At the moment she felt like a living oxymoron, frightened yet excited, torn from one thing to another, still there was nothing she could do about it. Somehow she knew the love she and Cary had professed to each other wasn't the only thing about to make her life change forever.

CHAPTER 10

Cary sat across from his mother on the small antique loveseat next to the woman he loved. Pat Jones' hand trembled when she placed the key into the old lock on the trunk.

He was glad Shannon temporarily closed Revamped. Especially after his mother said she only wanted a few people to know about what she was going to reveal. The older woman took a deep breath as if to calm herself, and he felt sorry for her. She had always been there for him, so he knew whatever she held secret would be hard for her to reveal.

"Cary, Hayley, when your father passed away two years ago, you know how much I missed him." Tears twinkled in her eyes as she removed the lock and unlatched the case. "I still do, but I want you to know, I knew nothing about the things I'm about to show you."

She pulled a piece of paper from her pocket. "I have to read this to you then we'll go on to the belongings of the trunk. I found this note in some of your dad's things, along with the key to this lock, and another key."

Cary watched as his mother placed a very old looking key on the table. He then saw Hayley shift in her chair as if she knew what the piece went to. Shannon reached over and picked up the small metal object.

Turning it over in her hand, she studied it. "Mrs. Jones, I think this key goes to the lock on the antique glass cabinet over there that belonged to the Rheas."

Hayley nodded. "That's what I thought, Shannon."

"You girls are right, that's precisely the lock it opens." Pat unfolded the paper in her hand.

Frowning Hayley said, "But I thought there was only one key to that lock."

"Let me read this. It will explain a lot." Pat placed her glasses on her nose.

"My beautiful wife, I know you've found the keys. Let me explain. I want you to know, you are the love of my life. You have stood at my side through thick and thin, but if you're reading this, now you stand alone.

"This isn't going to be easy, my love, but it's something I had to do for our family. You and I have both wondered for years if Cary was Clifford Rhea, reincarnated."

Shannon's gasp tore Cary's attention from his mother. Had he heard the woman right? They thought he was Clifford? He put his arm around Shannon's shoulder. "Mom, don't—"

Pat held up her hand. "Now, Cary, let me finish before you jump to conclusions. Please?"

He felt Shannon tremble beneath his embrace and pulled her tighter. "Shannon?"

She leaned into him. "I want to hear it all. Get this out in the open so it can be over with."

Pat nodded and continued, "In the wedding picture we have of the Rhea's, Clifford bears a striking resemblance to our son, but after in-depth research, I now can tell you why.

"You, my dear, are Clifford and Willena's great, great niece. Your great-great grandmother was Clifford Rhea's sister."

Hayley placed her hand over her mother's. "You mean we are ancestors of the Rheas,

Mom?"

Patting her daughter's hand, Pat said, "That's right, honey, we are."

"How exciting! I knew there was something about those people I loved, Now I know why. We're kin to them."

The sparkle in Cary's sister's eyes showed real happiness. However, he didn't know how to take the news. How long had his father known? "Mom, why didn't Dad tell us about this?"

His mother looked down at the hand she held the paper in, and with her free hand, twisted the wedding band she still wore. "There's a lot more to it than a simple explanation, honey. Your father, God rest his soul, being the town's historian, had access to records that weren't available to the general public. He found some that had been put aside and apparently forgotten."

She held the letter out in front of her and began to read again. "I discovered some old immigration papers in the courthouse basement. Clifford and Willena's and your grandmother's were among them. Cliff's sister's name was Sarah. The documents had been discarded for some odd reason, but I salvaged them, and you'll find them in the root cellar under the Rhea building."

"Root cellar?" Cary couldn't believe what

he was hearing.

"Yes, honey, and there's a way to get to it from the storeroom of this building."

That was impossible. Cary knew every inch of this old building. He'd surely know if there was a door in the storeroom leading to a root cellar. "I've never seen anything that could lead under the building. Maybe Dad was mistaken."

Shaking her head, Pat said, "No, there's no mistake. Your father found out about the old cellar when he found the drawing that Clifford Rhea had made of how he was going to build this place. It included the cellar and the apartment above."

This was almost too much to take in at one time. He could only imagine how Shannon felt. He glanced at her and she was totally focused on Pat. When Dane chimed, Cary looked up to see Johnny Franklin enter, then close the door behind him. His father's longtime friend approached without a word.

He met Shannon's gaze. "I thought you locked that door."

"I did, too. I know I put the closed sign up."

Pat smiled at the older man and laid the letter aside. "Perfect timing, John, have a seat."

Cary stood and reached to shake Johnny's

hand. "Good to see you."

"I was rather surprised to get your mother's call this morning." He accepted Cary's handshake then sat in a vacant chair.

Returning to his place beside Shannon, he took her hand and glanced at his mother. "It seems she's full of surprises as of late."

"Yes, well." Pat cleared her throat. "As I told you kids last night, I've been waiting for a good while to get this all out in the open. So, I wanted Johnny to know, too."

"Know what?" Johnny looked at the box on the table. "Is that Jones' old trunk?"

Pat nodded. "Yes. Okay, everyone please let me finish."

Listening while his mother filled Johnny in on what she'd been telling them, Cary began to let it all sink in. But there was still so much that didn't make since. Hidden rooms, historical records, immigrants, and they were kin to the Rheas? He only hoped when all was said and done, he'd understand.

"Johnny, my husband dug a tunnel many years ago that is a passageway to the root cellar."

"A passageway, Mother?" Cary could tell by the look on Johnny's face that the man was also having a hard time with all of this.

"Yes, son. According to your father's letter, the owners that bought this building, after my uncle died, didn't want to use the cellar, so they simply closed it up by covering the stairway with flooring.

"On one of the occasions when the building was empty, your father cut some of the plank flooring out and made an opening so he could get in and out of the building without anyone's knowledge. That's how he got some of these things." Pat opened the trunk.

Had his father been the one taking items from the previous owners over the years? He didn't want to believe that, but all fingers pointed to that very thing.

Cary vowed to find the secret hiding place beneath the building, but now, he wanted to see what was among his father's belongings. On top of the contents lay Cary's dad's army uniform and hat. He'd been through these things a hundred times when he was younger, and that's exactly how he remembered them lying every time. "What things, Mother?"

She pulled out the uniform, put it to her nose and took a deep breath then placed it beside her. Beneath it was an old frame. He imagined it was the Rhea's wedding photo as she lay the frame face down on the uniform.

"All of these things originally belonged to Clifford and Willena Rhea."

Cary sat forward and gazed into the trunk. Trinkets, a beautiful old dress, some pictures and a small wooden box, among other things, were inside.

CHAPTER 11

Shannon stood and started to reach into the trunk then paused. "May I, Mrs. Jones?"

Pat pushed the trunk closer to her. "Of course."

Her heart raced as she touched the fabric of the very old, off-white dress. It was simple, yet elegant and she fell in love with it immediately. Not knowing how fragile the material might be, she tried to be gentle as she pulled it out. "Isn't this lovely?"

Letting it fall to its full length, she realized what it was. "This is Willena's wedding gown, isn't it?" A smile lifted the corners of

Pat Jones' lips.

"Indeed it is. My husband and I bought it, and the Rhea's wedding picture, right after we married. We stopped at a small antique dealer's shop while we were on our honeymoon. Something drew my husband to the items and he wouldn't leave without them. We didn't know until we took the frame off of the picture to look for markings that it was the Rheas. You can imagine how we felt."

"Amazing." The story was wonderful, but it didn't touch the beauty of the garment she held. It was soft, pliable and still had the scent of perfume on it. No, that was only her imagination. "This cloth is over 150 years old and it still looks new! It's been so well preserved." Careful not to let the fabric touch the ground, she folded the dress back the way it was and placed it on the couch where she'd been sitting.

There were so many items in the trunk; she didn't know what to look at next. Then she noticed a small wooden box. It was amongst everything else, but it seemed to stand out.

No matter how hard she tried, she couldn't quiet the tremble of her hand when she reached for the box. She realized Cary now stood beside her, and when he placed his arm around her waist, calm swept over her and the trembling subsided.

"Want me to get it?"

His voice soothed her even further. Every emotion she'd ever felt, again ran rampant through her. It had to be the anticipation of having these treasures in front of her.

She wasn't sure what rested inside the little package, but in her heart, she knew it was something precious. She swallowed the lump in her throat and nodded. Cary reached into his father's trunk and carefully picked up the box. Shannon paid attention when Pat began to read again.

"There are other items in the root cellar as well.

"When you read this, you will know who has been taking the items from the Rhea building all these years. I couldn't stand to see these historical things leave our little community, and when we were younger, you and I could have never afforded to buy them all. Please, forgive me.

"Please tell my son and daughter I love them very much and now that they know the secret, I hope they can forgive me, too.

"Pat, I hated lying to you, but you would have tried to stop me, and I felt compelled to continue."

Shannon listened in stunned silence to Ben Jones' words. The man had been the one that had stolen the items. The look on Cary's face told her it was something he never thought his dad would do, but the truth lay in front of him, and there was more beneath the building. Her heart went out to the man she loved.

Pat wiped a tear from her cheek, reached into the bottom of the trunk and pulled out a manila envelope. She continued to read. "However, you will find money, the names, phone numbers and addresses of everyone who owned the things I took. There should be enough to pay for each item. Then these treasures will truly belong to you and the kids to do with what you want.

"The key to the lock on the Rhea's cabinet is in there as well. I had it made many years ago. That's how I gained access to the case." Pat stopped and held the letter out.

"Here, Cary, I can't read anymore. I've read it a hundred times and know it by heart."

He took the paper from his mother and read the rest to himself. Hayley and John comforted Pat while Shannon reached for the picture that still lay face down on the uniform. Pat touched her hand and she met the older woman's gaze.

"Are you sure you're ready to see that?"

Of course she wanted to look at it. Why would Pat even ask such a thing? She nodded and Pat released her grasp, picked up the photo and handed it to her.

Her breath caught in her throat when she saw the faded image. It couldn't be. Her knees were going to buckle beneath her. Cary's voice calling her name echoed in the distance and the world around her faded to black.

Damp coolness washed over Shannon's face and neck. She felt comfortable and safe, but what had happened? The ringing in her ears quieted and she heard a man and woman talking. Everything became clearer and she was suddenly in reality.

"Shannon? Shannon?"

Cary's voice was filled with concern ,and when she opened her eyes he was sitting on the edge of the bed. Her own bed and Cary wiped her face with a wet cloth while Hayley stood behind him and gazed at her with worried eyes.

She forced the words out but wasn't sure she wanted to know. "What happened? How did I get upstairs?"

Cary bent and kissed her. Gentle, caring, yet passionate, and she welcomed it. Then she heard Hayley clear her throat.

"Ummm… welcome back."

Cary released her lips, straightened and met

her gaze. "I carried you up here after you fainted when you saw the photo of Clifford and Willena."

The memory came flooding back. "Oh, my gosh! It's us, Cary. That's us in that picture." Could it be they were really the Rheas reincarnated? It went against every logical thing her father had instilled in her, however she couldn't help but wonder.

A shiver ran up her spine. Had she lived before? Is that why she fell in love with Cary instantly? She couldn't bring herself to look away from his green eyes. The man she loved reassured her with his smile.

"I admit, at first glance, the resemblance is uncanny, but you have to remember Clifford's blood runs in my veins. I do look like him, but that's not me in that picture." He handed her the photo.

She was almost afraid to look at it again, but she forced herself. Amazed at the resemblance between Clifford and Cary, she now saw the differences. However, she was even more astounded at her likeness to Willena. "That's all well and good but what about—"

"You looking like Willie? I don't know, but we might find the answer in the documents in the cellar."

Hayley stepped forward. "Speaking of the

cellar, and now that I know you're okay, I'm going to go see what Mom and John have found down there."

CHAPTER 12

Shannon glanced at the engagement ring on her finger. Soon it would be coupled with Willena's gold wedding band and she and Cary would be married.

"Only five minutes before you walk down the aisle and become my sister-in-law." Hayley straightened Shannon's veil.

"Shannon," Pat said. "You look stunning in that dress. Willena would be proud to know you are wearing it. Such a perfect fit."

It *was* a perfect fit, and this was a perfect day, the day she would become the man of her dreams' wife. She felt really beautiful for the first time in her life. "Thank you."

"Not only does it look spectacular on you, but it will go perfect on the manikin in the new museum." Pat dabbed at her eyes with a tissue. "I only wish Ben was here to see all of this."

Hayley put her arm around her mother's shoulder. "He would be pleased at the way things panned out."

Shannon was ecstatic that she and Cary made the decision to turn the Rhea building into the Rhea Museum. She still couldn't believe none of the previous owners would take any money for the items that had belonged to them, but instead, donated it all to the Museum.

Even though she owned the Rhea building, she didn't feel she had the right to any of the things in the trunk or what they found in the cellar. The only things they kept were the Rheas' wedding rings. Her heart soared when the Crawford's insisted on it; after all, they bought the rings originally and were the rightful owners, so she graciously accepted.

The empty wooden box that once held the precious gold would sit in the original Rhea's cabinet. She had a plaque made stating gratitude and thanks to the couple for their gift. Hayley's voice pulled her from her thoughts.

"I'm just glad we found out you're not our long-lost cousin or something."

"Me, too. If that would have been the case, I wouldn't be marrying your brother today and you wouldn't be my maid of honor."

They'd done hours of research and found it was simply coincidental that her late husband's name was Rhea and that she resembled Willena. Thanks to her dad's teachings, she'd stayed grounded through everything that had happened. She knew there had to be logical explanations.

Well, for everything except Dane. He rang more merrily than ever these days. Maybe it just seemed that way because she was so happy. The world was brighter, and the weight of her previous life was lifted from her shoulders, never to return.

"I think it's kind of funny Cary made Johnny pay up on their bet." Hayley smiled.

What was she talking about? "Bet? What kind of bet?"

"John said you wouldn't make it to tourist season before you ran away from the Rhea building. He bet Cary a hundred dollars on it. I'm really glad my brother won."

She looked at her soon-to-be sister-in-law and mother-in-law. They'd welcomed her into the family, and she was grateful for their acceptance. "Me, too."

The door opened and Cassie Franklin entered with a grin. "It's time, ladies." She approached Pat. "Mrs. Jones, Papa John's waiting to walk you down the aisle and get you seated, then he'll join Cary at the front of the church. Hayley, you go next then take your place at the alter across from Papa John."

The young lady had helped so much in the planning of the wedding and had taken control of the food. Franklins was catering the reception, and Shannon was impressed at how organized Cassie was. Shannon saw a sweet smile cross Cassie's face.

"Cary's waiting for you, Miss Shannon. Are you ready?"

She was more ready than she ever thought possible. She followed the others then stood in the doorway leading into the small chapel.

Her heart wouldn't stop pounding. Within the next few minutes she would be Mrs. Cary Jones. She never thought she'd find true love, but she couldn't deny it had happened.

Looking up, she met his gaze. His mesmerizing green eyes took her to another place and everything around her disappeared. At that moment, she felt as if only she and Cary existed in the world, her world, no, their world.

He was the most handsome man she'd ever seen. Standing tall and proud, he winked at her. That's all it took for her knees to become weak. The pure excitement of knowing she'd be in his arms in a few short hours released an abundance of butterflies in her stomach. Heat rose to her cheeks in anticipation of what the night would hold.

"Shannon."

Cassie's whisper drew her from her private thoughts, and she realized the wedding march was playing. She stepped into the chapel and walked down the aisle toward her man. His smile warmed her heart and the twinkle in his eye said he looked forward to their wedding night, too.

The pastor's words all but faded into the distance as she concentrated on the love of her life. He was everything she'd ever wanted.

Something had drawn her to this little town, to Cary Jones. Everything proved to be logical, but she couldn't deny there was at least something a little mystical about their love. Whatever it was, she wouldn't question it.

"The rings, please." The pastor took the rings from John. "These golden bands represent the eternal circle of love. They are special in more ways than one but now they will forever belong to Shannon and Cary." He handed Shannon one of the bands. "Place this on Cary's finger and repeat after me."

Her voice came out barely above a whisper. She didn't care, the only one who needed to hear her was Cary. Tears welled in his eyes as she repeated the sacred vows and pushed the ring into place.

The preacher gave Cary the remaining band. "Cary, place this on Shannon's finger and repeat after me."

Cary took her left hand in his and placed the golden ring, which represented his eternal love, on her finger. She closed her eyes as a tear slid down her cheek. She loved this man far beyond anything she could have imagined.

"You may kiss your bride."

Applause broke out and echoed throughout the room when Cary took her mouth with his. When his lips left hers, he held her tight. His breathy whisper was warm, but his words sent a shiver of delight down her spine.

"Our lives have been…revamped."

OTHER BOOKS BY SHARON

Autobiography
Following Daddy's Footsteps: My Life in the Music Business

Biographical Fiction
The Will and the Wisp
A Star that Twinkled but Never got to Shine

Steamy Romance
Ride the Storm
Gamble for Life

Sweet Romance
The Cowboy and Emily Tipton
Bottom's Up
No Room to Spare
The Ride of a Lifetime
Christmas Gifts from God

Children's Books
My Forever Friend (Tail Wags Book 1)
Children Did You Know: Santa Believes (w/companion coloring book)
Children Did You Know: Easter Bunny Believes (w/companion coloring book)

Camouflage Santa Claus (w/companion coloring book)

Kindle Only
Paranormal Short Stories

ABOUT THE AUTHOR

Sharon Kizziah-Holmes is a retired professional musician. She and her husband lived on the road playing honky tonks in Alaska, Canada and the lower forty-eight states. Now, she lives in the beautiful Ozarks with her husband Dennis and dogs, Willie and Waylon.

She has been an indie-author since 2002 and is well versed in the self-publishing industry. She is the co-founder and co-owner of Paperback Press LLC., with imprints Paperback Press, Kids Book Press, Indie Pub Press and Audio Book Press.

She has served as publishing coordinator to over 150 authors, assisting in publishing 500 plus books for writers in the US and abroad. Several have become bestselling, self-published authors.

A board member of Ozarks Creative Writers Conference, Co-Chair and conference coordinator of Between the Pages Writers Con and President of Ozarks Romance authors, Sharon also remains active in many other writers' groups.